'TIS SO SUITE

Tales of an Innkeeper

Kathy Branning

ISBN 978-1-68570-096-6 (paperback)
ISBN 978-1-68570-097-3 (digital)

Christian Faith Publishing
832 Park Avenue
Meadville, PA 16335
www.christianfaithpublishing.com

Printed in the United States of America

What you focus on, you create more of.

1

I get out of bed when the alarm goes off at 5:30 a.m., and I head to the bathroom to pee. I throw on a sports bra and some leggings and head to the kitchen for a glass of water and a banana. As I reach for my banana, I can see Grandma is out for her morning swim. My mom moved in with us a while ago, and she lives in the mother-in-law suite on the other side of the pool just along the row of fruit trees. She loves her morning swims; better than a cup of coffee, she says.

I sit with my water and banana as I spend some time reading my Bible before my 6:00 a.m. workout. It is brutal, but I love how strong and capable my body feels, even if I haven't had any coffee yet.

Alan, my husband, joins me for my workout occasionally and provides a little competitive edge—playfully, of course. Him being six foot three and having grown up athletic gives him a leg up sometimes, but I'm a scrappy underdog who never gives up. I finished the core circuit a minute before he does. Victory! I have just enough time to hop in the shower before Alan. Ha! Beat him again.

I catch Jessica before she runs out the door.

"Bye, sweetie! Have a good day at school!" I yell after her.

"Love you, Mom!" she yells back.

She is so self-sufficient; it is as impressive as it is shocking. When did she get so grown up? She's so tall, just like a model, with her long blond hair and big blue eyes and an even bigger heart.

After sufficiently showering off my workout grime, I throw on some makeup and put on the outfit I hung out for myself last night: my favorite jeans and a teal sweater to match my eyes. I choose my low-heeled booties because truth be told, I'm quite tall enough without heels.

Last but not least, the hair! I have a lot of thick red hair, and sometimes, I find myself wishing it was more low maintenance or that I was the type who could rock an unkempt two-second messy bun, but I actually really do love my hair. I love curling it; I love straightening it; it is one of my favorite things about myself.

Down in loose curls today, in case you were wondering. I double-check I have all my things; give Alan a kiss goodbye; grab my little bichon frise, Molly; and head to the inn.

*****

As I pull up to Still Waters Inn, I get that familiar ting of gratitude. I take a moment to thank God that I get to live my dream of owning and running my own inn. Still Waters, my inn, is a beautiful newly remodeled Victorian bed-and-breakfast-themed place of refuge for weary travelers who come to be refreshed by our homey, welcoming atmosphere. I still have to pinch myself to be sure this is all real, even though it took a lot of hard work and perseverance to get here.

I head straight to the kitchen for my morning coffee and some breakfast. Making the decision to serve breakfast at the inn was genius, if I do say so myself. We also serve freshly baked pastries—provided by my daughter, Jessica, and myself—and coffee any way you want it.

Obviously, coffee is a high priority for me. Did I tell you I owned and ran a coffee shop when I was younger? It was an awesome experience, but I was a young mother with a young kiddo who needed me more than the coffee drinkers of our town did.

I check in with my chef and best friend to see how the breakfast rush is going.

"Everyone wanted waffles today!" exclaims Nikki. "Is there something in the air? I've been making waffles since I got in early this morning. Please tell me you want your usual and not waffles too."

"As tempting as waffles sound," I respond, "my usual avocado and egg on sourdough is just fine.

"It must be the crisp fall air," I add. "Did you see the trees this morning? The colors are starting to turn. I'm going to really enjoy taking Molly out for her walk later. Don't you just love the smell of fall?"

"Your obsession with fall is just a little out there, don't you think?" asks Nikki.

"Are you kidding me?" I ask. "Fall is magical! Pumpkin everything, scarves, boots, sweaters, the leaves, the colors, the weather..."

"I get it. I get it! How much coffee did you have this morning?" exclaims Nikki. "Now, go eat your breakfast, and get out of here before people start requesting pumpkin pancakes."

*****

I sit down in my office thinking about the pumpkin pancakes I'm going to beg Sally for tomorrow morning and finish my coffee while I go over my day. I'm what some people call type A: I love lists, planners, and organization. Going over my planner is one of my favorite things. Dorky, I know!

Looks like I've got some emails to respond to, supervise checkout at noon, have lunch with Brianne followed up by a meeting at 2:00 p.m. before heading home for the day. I take my final sip of coffee just as my sweet Molly scratches at the patio door. Time for our morning walk around the property.

I love bringing my sweet pup to work with me, and the guests who stay here love her big brown eyes, sweet smile, and furiously wagging tail. Thankfully, she's a hypoallergenic breed, so we don't have to worry about anyone having an allergic reaction.

Today is a perfect day for a walk; day in and day out, it's the same route, but when the weather shifts and it's gloriously brisk out, it makes for a picture-perfect walk. It reminds me of something I read out of a poetry book:

> The autumn has dressed herself for the
> coming season, donning her most vibrant hues.
> She has swept into our streets and woodlands

with a humble boldness that invited the eye to see more than they otherwise might. The autumn takes her pirouette, her sweet turn on the stage all around, and we are so blessed to be given such beauty.

Okay, maybe I *am* obsessed.

After greeting some of our guests—who had the same idea for a delightful autumn walk—and allowing Ms. Molly to do her business, it was time to check in with the staff and make sure that no one needed anything. This inn is a smooth-sailing ship, but every now and then, someone needs me a little extra. Like that time Mr. and Mrs. Holiday tried to smuggle out the inn towels from every room or we unexplainably ran out of all our pillow chocolates—three weeks' worth!

But today, thankfully, is not one of those days; everything seems to be going like clockwork. I take another moment to thank God for His goodness.

*****

After completing my morning tasks, I see the final guest checking out and wish them well as I head out to the gazebo to have lunch with Brianne.

"Hey, Brianne! What did you bring us today?" I ask.

"Turkey wrap for you and a vegan wrap for me, and butternut squash soup for both of us."

Brianne proudly provided the lunch fare, and I pulled out two ice-cold La Croix. Brianne is one of those extremely kind and generous people whom if you're lucky enough to befriend you have a friend for life.

"So how was your honeymoon?" I ask. "Did you and Rich love Greece?"

"Greece was so magical," Brianne responds dreamily. "You have to go. Rich and I had such a good time. I loved the vineyards and oceanside. It was like being in a fairy tale."

"I know I've said it a million times, but I'm so happy for you!" I exclaim.

After enjoying a yummy, nutritious lunch and catching up on life, I say goodbye to Brianne yet again as she jet sets around the country to provide care for those in need. She has launched her interior design line at Target—move over, Magnolia—but she still feels called to serve people through her travel nursing or client care and has a new, loving, and vibrant marriage. Brianne's wedding was one of the firsts we hosted at Still Waters Inn, and it was breathtaking.

Thankful for a productive and peaceful day at work, me and Molly head home. As I walk into our two-story cobblestone home with a teal front door, Molly runs ahead of me and greets Jessica with kisses (or as we like to call them, *blehs*).

*****

"Hey, kiddo!" I say. "How was school?"

"It was fine," she responded, much like every other day.

"Highs and lows?" I prod.

"Lola invited me and some other girls to the lake on Saturday in their family's boat—can I go?—and we had math."

"Yes, you can go, and you have math every day," I respond with a laugh.

"Yeah, but it's still a low…thanks, Mom! I'm going to go finish my homework so I can play cards with Grandma."

I stop by Alan's home office on my way to the kitchen to give him a quick kiss before I start dinner. Stuffed bell peppers—a family favorite, and it's easy and nutritious, my favorite combo. After dinner, my mom generously does the dishes, as she does every night. She insists, and since it used to be Alan's chore, he's thrilled to let her do it. Jessica runs over to the inn to bake her famous snickerdoodle cookies for tomorrow's guest, and Alan and I take Molly for her evening walk and to watch the sunset. This was the perfect autumn day.

After Jessica and my mom retire for the evening, Alan and I sit in our chairs and catch up on our day.

"How are the companies doing?" I ask. "Was it a good day?"

"It was a great day, Kate. All our companies are rocking and rolling. Your inn is booked solid for the rest of the year. We might think about expanding it."

"I don't know, babe. That's a big step. Do you think we are ready?" I question.

"Where's that mindset of abundance?" Alan asks.

"Ha ha! You're right."

Next thing I know, Alan is on his feet pulling me to mine. I suddenly realize there is music playing. Crooner music. A little Sinatra is always welcome.

As we dance into the night, I take a moment to thank God for this incredible life. Thank you, Jesus, that You came so we could live life to the fullest. Then I look into Alan's eyes, and I see that familiar twinkle.

"Are you ready for bed?" he asks with a wink.

"Yes, I am."

2

My dream of owning my own inn slowly blossomed into frui-
tion over the course of four or five years. See, I used to own
a coffee shop; it was called Kate's Kafe. I felt it was my Proverbs 31
vineyard ("She considers a field and buys it; out of her earnings she
plants a vineyard" [Proverbs 31:16].).

I knew I could do it. I didn't know why. I had no previous
knowledge or experience, but I gave it my all. It was a passion proj-
ect, and it was successful. I loved coffee, I loved people, and it was a
great merger to live fully with both.

I purchased my coffee from an above–fair trade farm in Rwanda
that helps the people of the land rebuild their lives and supports
other social justice causes around the world. It sure did not hurt that
the coffee was delicious. I had a truly clear vision for my coffee shop:
it would be a place of refuge, with a peaceful atmosphere set by con-
tinuous worship music, mostly Jesus Culture.

I loved the idea of my shop being a meeting place for people to
come together, break bread, and enjoy community in my little refuge
tucked away behind the main boulevard. It was a wonderful outlet
for my love of baking; now I could bake to my heart's desire and not
have the temptation of eating it all. There is nothing like having the
immediate satisfaction of watching someone else enjoy something
you created—whether it was a paleo doughnut, a krackle, or a dirty
pumpkin latte.

I had my early-morning regulars who stopped on their way to
work. I had the local businessmen who stopped in for a jolt of java.
I had mom groups, church groups, study groups, and friend groups.
Most of my business came from the bustling salon next door. I'd
send Jessica over in her tiny apron and a tray of samples, and she'd

come back with a list of orders for me to fill. She was only three at the time and loved being my little barista. She would go around to customers and ask them if they needed a napkin or straws; the customers ate it up!

The thing I did not consider was that I would be working from 5:00 a.m. to 9:00 p.m. six days a week. Having a toddler and with no one to really watch out for her, things got tricky. It got to the point where it was too busy for me to handle on my own but not busy enough to hire enough staff to allow me to be home with my energetic kiddo. I loved the idea of raising children in a business, having her grow up with an entrepreneurial spirit and a great work ethic, but I could see that something was not right.

After two years, I felt it was time for me to hang up my apron. I never saw it as a failure; I knew I was choosing the right thing. It felt more like I was hitting the pause button.

People would ask me all the time if I was going to open another coffee shop. My response was always "If not a coffee shop, something like a coffee shop." I knew I wasn't done; I just wasn't convinced it would look the same. I learned some particularly important lessons in business in those two years, and a short time later, my dream of my inn started blossoming. I protected it, shielded it, shared this sacred dream only with a precious few. I was nervous, how could I do something so huge, people would think I was a joke, it made my chest beat far too hard, and the excitement it instilled in me was far too huge.

But the more I allowed myself to dream about my inn and the more I allowed others into this dream, the closer I got to making it happen. My belief system started to shift from "Something that would be nice but probably not going to happen" to "I was born for this; what are the steps I need to take to make this dream a reality?"

Thus began the real journey, the hard work, the boots to the ground. I researched. I made a vision board. I received encouragement and affirmation to keep going from my community. I would not have gotten here without my village, and even if I did, it would have been longer and much harder. A good community who will build you up is worth more than gold. I am one blessed woman— rich with love, friendship, and support.

And that, my dears, is how it all began.

*****

Today is Friday; that means we have the wedding to finish preparing the inn for before tomorrow morning. I mean, really, who has a sunrise wedding?

"Nikki, that cake looks gorgeous!" I exclaim as I pour myself a cup of coffee. "How did you get all the colors of a sunrise on that cake like that?"

"It's just a simple ombré cake," Nikki responds. "I kind of wish it was more of a challenge, actually."

"Okay, master chef, do you have everything you need for the hors d'oeuvres and brunch items? I have to run to the market for a few items. I can grab something for you, if you need."

Brunch at a wedding. Okay, that is an idea I can get behind.

"I *hope* I have everything I need," answers Nikki. "Otherwise I'm going to be sobbing. No ugly crying for all to see and hear. I cannot believe how many times your mom has changed the menu."

"I know. It's just that she wants it to be perfect this time. She has waited so long since my dad to even consider remarrying. I think she gets a little nervous sometimes."

My mom is getting married tomorrow; that also means she is moving out this weekend. So many little things, loose ends to tie up and so many feelings. I am happy for her, I really am. She deserves to be happy. She had to endure so much in her life. It is nice to see things in her life falling into place.

I'm not gonna lie, things have been tense at home lately. I know that her emotions have been getting stirred up, and so have mine. I love Henry. He is perfect for my mom, and he is so sweet and gentle with her. But this wedding makes me think of my dad, all the things he wasn't—for me, for her. There's no denying the things he did give us: for me, it's my eyes, my love for singing, and all things music and cheesy jokes, and for her, she got me...ha ha, I know, I know.

I am a little bit vain; I got that from him too. But he was a mean husband and an absent father. I look at Henry and see how happy he makes my mom and how comfortable I am with him, and wonder why I couldn't have had him as my father in the first place.

Party of one, please. Okay, pity party over.

I know it's pathetic. I know that my life is really great and I'm literally living my dream, but sometimes, I think of the little girl that I used to be, and I feel the hollow pain that kept her company for so long, and grief hits me like a semi coming down the I-5.

I have been seeing a counselor for a while, and it has really helped, but she also encouraged me to let the grief come so that I can move forward and heal. Not to try and distract myself with busyness and tasks like I used to do but be sad and feel the pain, because whether I want it or not it is there. So I either deal with it when it comes or lose sleep because I am woken up by bad dreams or anxiety attacks, neither of which makes me very productive the following day anyhow.

In any case, before my mom and Henry got engaged, I thought I was done grieving because I had been great for months, although in hindsight it may have just been the high from opening the inn and all the hubbub and excitement that came with. It is so interesting that one of the biggest times of my life is accompanied by some of the biggest healing that has ever come in my life. I really am thankful, even if it does hurt. I know that I am making progress and growing and becoming a more whole version of myself. I just don't feel like it at the moment.

*****

"Hi, Mom!" I say as I walk through the door. "Are you ready for your big day?"

"I went to the beauty school this morning to get my hair tinted and my nails done," my mom says. "Are you sure you don't mind curling it before the ceremony?"

"Of course, Mom. I love that I get to do your hair. Do you need anything else?" I ask.

"Katelyn…"

My mother is the only one who calls me that besides telemarketers.

"You need to stop fussing over me," Mom said. "I'm a grown woman who used to change *your* diapers. I'm perfectly capable of taking care of myself."

"Okay, okay. Just checking. You know I can't help myself!" I exclaim. "By the way, I love the color you chose for you nails, very chic."

"Thank you." Then she asks, "Are you sure you're okay with this? Okay with me marrying Henry?"

"Of course! I love Henry!" I gush. "I wish you could have gone to Diamond Fellowship and met him sooner."

We both laugh so hard we are doubled over. Diamond Fellowship is this great little senior group over at the church. They get together every week for potlucks, worship, and card games—three of my mom's favorite things. That is where Henry first stole my mom's heart. I always give him a hard time—"Really, Henry, stealing at church?" They really are two peas in a pod, and since they are both well into their seventies, they deserve to have companionship and spend the rest of their days exactly as they wish.

"Mom?"

"Yes, Katelyn?"

"Are you happy?" I ask.

"Yes, honey, I really am," my mom replies.

"Good. I'm glad. You deserve to be, Mom."

I hug her tightly as tears threaten to spring out from behind my tightly squeezed eyelids.

I grab the hot curling iron and start on her strawberry blond hair. I love it when my mom—or Jessica, for that matter—let me style their hair for special occasions. It is so fun to glam them up a little and especially today. And especially my mom.

"Ouch!" I yell, and kiss my finger—again. "Okay, I'm awake now!"

"Honey, be careful. Maybe you should let Jessica take over with my hair so you don't keep burning yourself," Mom advises.

"No, it's okay. I'm almost done. I promise I won't burn myself again," I reply, as Jessica rolls her eyes at me. "At least not this morning."

"Mom, you always burn yourself on that curling wand," Jessica accuses.

"You look radiant this morning, Mom," I say to my mom, changing the subject. "But remind me again why you chose to get married so early in the morning?"

"Oh, you stinker! You know this is our favorite time of the day, Henry and I," Mom replies. "And our first date was getting up to watch the sun rise together."

*****

As I walk down the aisle and stand up on the steps of the twinkle-light-adorned gazebo for my mom—just me, her matron of honor, and Ali, her bridesmaid—I take in the beauty of my surroundings.

The rich greenery that has already started fading into beautiful autumnal hues of oranges, golds, and reds. The gorgeous two-toned peach roses, soft-pink carnations, and pale-yellow daisies my mom chose for her wedding flowers. The elegant yet simple touches of vintage lace lining the aisle. The early, glorious first golden rays of sunlight peeking out above the horizon. The rays touch the curves of the mountains in the distance with a color of their own. Even as a self-described "not morning person," I can say there can be nothing more pleasing to the senses or as romantic than the sunrise. Nature is at its best at this heavenly hour. The golden rays of the sun give a bright coloring to the clouds and meadows, mountains, and valleys.

Turning my attention to the beginning of the wedding march followed by my beautiful mom ascending down the aisle, I just cannot hold it in. As she steps up onto the gazebo where her sweet Henry and Pastor Todd stood awaiting her arrival, the tears spring forth, and Jessica shoves out a tissue toward my hand.

"I knew you'd cry," Jessica teases.

I don't think I've seen my mom ever look so happy in my whole life. Her dress flows around her like she was an angel, with its soft ivory satin and lace trim, complimenting her peachy complexion and the stunning job Ali did on her natural but classy makeup that made her green eyes pop. It is her time; for me to see God's redemption in her life is one of the sweetest gifts I could ever ask for. My mom sacrificed so much for my brother and I; it was her time.

"Ladies and gentlemen, family and friends," the pastor says. "We are gathered here today to witness and celebrate the joining of Betty Jean Thomas and Henry Samuel McGuire in marriage. With love and commitment, they have decided to live their lives together as husband and wife. Betty and Henry, may the Lord grant you the serenity to accept the things you cannot change, the courage to change the things you must, and the wisdom to know the difference. Live each day one at a time enjoying your time together, one moment at a time. Seek the wisdom of the Lord, learning all that you can from each other. Accept trials as joy, knowing that the testing of your faith produces patience. Trusting that the Lord will make all things right if you surrender to His will, that you would be reasonably happy in this life and supremely happy with Him forever in the next. Amen.

"Do you, Betty, take Henry to be your lawfully wedded husband, to have and to hold from this day forward, for better or worse, for richer, for poorer, in sickness and in health, to love and to cherish from this day forward, for as long as you both shall live?"

"I do," replies my mom.

"Do you, Henry, take Betty to be your lawfully wedded wife, to have and to hold from this day forward, for better or worse, for richer, for poorer, in sickness and in health, to love and to cherish from this day forward, for as long as you both shall live?"

"I do," replies Henry.

I try to stop crying and hold my breath so I could clearly take in every detail from the rest of the wedding, and I'm sure it was beautiful, and then at some point, I hear the pastor proclaim, "I now pronounce you husband and wife. You may now kiss the bride!"

Now the tears stop on their own. Watching your mom kiss a man—now *that* is something I never thought I'd have to get used to, but I welcome the awkward discomfort of the whole package. Mom's happy. What more could I ask for?

*****

"Are you ready for your speech?" Alan asks.

"I guess so," I answer.

I smooth the front of my blush gown, take another sip of coffee, head up to the stage, and take the microphone.

"There are a lot of sacrifices a mother makes when she's raising children by herself," I begin. "I saw it when I was growing up, watching all my mother did for me, but it wasn't until recent years that I fully understood the price she paid because of how we had to struggle. Mom, I am so happy for you. The road to get here was long, winding, and treacherous, but nevertheless, you got here. Your shared love for the Lord and each other is precious and a treat to behold. Henry, treat her well!

"Mom, I hope you feel beautiful. You deserve to be looking this young and radiant and full of joy, and I'm honored to be able to witness it firsthand. A moment like this and the commitment which follows should be celebrated to its fullest. And so I contend to all those present that it is our duty to ensure that this moment in the lives of my mom and Henry does not pass uncelebrated. It is with great pleasure that I say congratulations to mom and Henry. May you share your lifetime of love and happiness. Oh, and please let's not forget, a very happy birthday, Mom!"

Everyone raises their glass and cheers some form of "Congratappy birth cheers." I wipe the tears from my eyes and walk over to my mom and Henry. I give Henry a friendly hug and turn to my mom for one of her killer bear hugs.

"Oh, honey," she says with emotion in her voice. "That was so sweet. This is all too much. You've done too much."

"Mom, no way," I say. "It is definitely not too much. Henry, please tell your wife she deserves to be doted upon and made to feel special, especially on her birthday slash wedding day." I cross my arms and give my mom a silly look.

Henry wraps Mom up in his arms and says, "Betty, stop making a fuss. It's our turn to fuss over you—just for today now, don't get used to it." And with a wink, Henry gives her the sweetest little peck on the lips.

"Grandma! You look so pretty!" Jessica comes running over and slings an arm around her grandma.

"Thank you, sweetie," Grandma Betty says. "My, I can't believe what a beautiful woman you've become! Just look at you in that fuchsia dress."

"Okay," Henry says. "I'm gonna go over to the buffet before someone tells me how pretty my dress is. There is a little too much gushing happening over here."

As Henry walks over to the buffet, my brother, Matthew, and his family come up to greet Mom.

"Congratulations, Mom. Oh! And happy birthday too, it was really nice," Matthew says.

"Thank you, son," Mom replies. "Now let me squeeze my grandbabies."

"Grandma!" groans Jake, my brother's teen son. "We aren't babies anymore!"

"Yeah, Grandma, we love you, and you look so pretty and your hair and your dress," says Ellen, my brother's sweet little girl. "Oh yeah, and happy birthday!"

"Ellen, take a breath, dear." Mom laughs.

Everyone is smiling and laughing and having a good time; it is just as it should be. What a beautiful moment of celebration, unity, and God's goodness.

I take another moment to thank God, this time for family, redemption, and His never-ending grace. Today marks not just my mom's birthday or wedding day but also a day of growth, a day of new, fresh hope for a bright future.

*****

As the wedding winds down and the crew starts cleaning up, I feel a droplet hit my forehead. I wipe it off, shake my head. It can't be. It's way too early for rain, and it isn't in the forecast.

I run inside to grab the umbrellas. Maybe some things can be salvaged before it really starts to pour.

"Here!" I yell. "Whoever needs an umbrella, grab one, and try to get everything inside or under cover before it gets ruined!"

"You know, usually, I love rain, but it's not very helpful while cleaning up an outdoor wedding," Alan says.

Luckily, all the sound equipment has already been put away. The food is getting put away, and all the chairs and tables will survive a little water. Running an inn is a never-ending job, but boy, do I love it.

3

It has been two months since my mom and Henry's wedding. They are simply the cutest newlyweds! The inn has been booked solid, which means I've been pretty busy. Jessica's bichon gave birth to a new litter, and it feels like we've got a newborn all over again—well, I guess you can say four fluffy little newborns who are too cute for words. I'm a big fan of reflecting…and coffee…and reflecting while drinking coffee.

Alan walks into my office, and I finish my last gulp of my pumpkin oat milk cold brew.

"Babe, I just got off the phone with Jessica, and the puppies are missing," he cries.

"What!" I exclaim. "What do you mean they are missing?"

"Jessica said she got home from school and went straight in to check on the pups, and no sign of them anywhere," Alan explains.

"What about Sapphire?" I ask. Sapphire is the mama dog.

"Sapphire is home," Alan replies. "Just the puppies are gone. Jessica said Sapphire looks sad and keeps whining and barking at the back door. Come on, we need to get home and call the police. I'll drive."

*****

Alan pulled into the driveway, and we both jumped out of the car and ran into the house, looking for tiny white fluff balls all the while. After getting another account with a few more details from Jessica, we turned the whole house upside down, searching for the puppies while waiting for the police to show up.

"Mom, the police are here!" Jessica called out.

"Thank-you for coming, officer," I say, "We need to report a stolen litter of puppies. There are four of them, and they are only seven weeks old."

"Hi, I'm Officer Sherman. Do you have a ring doorbell or any security cameras on the premises?" asked the officer.

"Oh, my goodness we do! Why didn't we think of that sooner?" I exclaim.

"It's okay, ma'am. You all are in shock," replied Officer Sherman.

I pull up the camera footage on my phone, and we all huddle around to watch; luckily, we installed a camera on our back patio as well as our front in case of shenanigans.

"Of course, they'd be wearing a hoody!" Jessica yells.

"But at least it's a bright-colored hoody with a readable logo on it," responds Officer Sherman.

After giving the physical description of each puppy to the officer, he responded, "We will start the investigation and let you know if we find anything. Since we have limited ID on the thief, it might prove difficult. I suggest posting flyers and posting on social media, but I don't want to give any false promises."

"Oh yeah, and make sure to lock your back door. Even if your back gate is locked, someone could still hop it, which is most likely what this guy did."

Alan and I catch each other's eye as we close the door behind the officer.

"It's just devastating how someone can just come and steal your puppies," Jessica said. "I know they were going to go to new homes eventually anyway but not like this. It's really traumatic."

"I know, honey, but we need to pray and have hope that we'll find the puppies and that they are safe," I tell her.

Alan picks up Sapphire and sits on the couch with her in his lap. He scratches behind her ear, and she responds with loving kisses (licks). Sapphire is used to breeding and selling her puppies to loving homes, but dogs are very intuitive, and this time she knows something is not right. We had buyers lined up for all but one of the puppies, and Jessica was going to keep the fourth; her name is Poppy.

*****

That night is a long pitiful, sleepless night for all of us. Even for Sapphire, who would not leave her post by the back door. Eventually I get up and take Sapphire's bed out of Jessica's room and put it by the back door so she can get a little rest.

I figure now is as good a time as any to start working on the flyers; no one is sleeping tonight anyway, so I don't have to worry about waking anyone up with the *click-clacking* of the computer keys or the whirring of the printer. It is a good thing Jessica takes so many pictures of her pups. I thought to myself, *I have plenty to choose from.*

I sit down at the computer and pick a large font, add a clear picture of the pups, and send it to the printer. I share it to all my social media platforms and have everyone we know share it. Surely, I thought, with this many eyes out there helping us look, those puppies will be found. Jessica already let the buyers know the situation, so they are in on the hunt as they all have their hopes on buying their chosen puppy.

"Guys," Jessica says as she comes into our room at 4:00 a.m., "can we pray again? I'm so worried about those puppies getting hurt. I just want them to be safe."

"Of course, honey," I respond.

As we huddle together, Alan prays a simple prayer. "Lord, please bring those puppies home and keep them safe. Amen"

"Thanks, Dad."

"You're welcome, kiddo. We will find those puppies. I feel really sure about it," Alan says.

*****

My favorite part of the day at Still Waters is usually breakfast: the food, the coffee, and meaningful conversations with the guests.

But today, the mood seems stale and the atmosphere eerily silent. By now, all the guests have seen the missing posters and are aware of the situation. I plan on hosting a special afternoon tea today for the guests to brighten up the place and lift spirits.

"I have everything ready for the tea this afternoon: fresh-baked scones ready to go and three different kinds of tea sandwiches ready to be assembled and served," Nikki says. "Any news on the puppies yet?"

"Not yet," I answer. "I'm praying for a miracle. The buyers are getting antsy, and Jessica is so disappointed. She somehow feels it's her fault. She takes on too much responsibility. It makes my momma heart hurt."

"They *will* turn up," Nikki assures me. "Keep your hope up. Remember, 'And we know that in all things God works for the good of those who love Him, who have been called according to His purpose.' Romans 8:28."

"Thanks, Nikki," I say. "It's good to have that reminder sometimes. I better go check my emails and see if there is any news on the pups."

I take my cup of coffee with me to my office and start up my computer; sometimes, routine can be so comforting. I remember the Bible verse Nikki quoted to me, and it reminded me of my devotions from this morning: "Carry each other's burdens, and in this way, you will fulfill the law of Christ" (Galatians 6:2).

God has placed you exactly where you are right in this moment. The people in your circle, the family you have, and the circumstances you find yourself in are all part of God's plan for your life! So true, I am grateful for the people God's placed in my life. I am now even more determined to keep the faith and try and help Jessica stay positive.

My cell phone rings, and I look at the caller ID—it's Lynn! Thank goodness. Lynn is one of my favorite people on the planet. She has strong faith and tends to be very practical, and I can always count on her to set me straight. Unfortunately, she is all the way in Canada, so I sent her a message last night to let her know about the puppies and to pray.

"Hi, Lynn, thanks for calling," I say.

"Hi, Kate, how are you doing? How's Jessica holding up? Have you heard anything about the puppies yet?" she asks.

"I'm doing okay. I'm keeping my hope up and trusting God. Jessica is taking it pretty hard, especially as the buyers she had lined up for the puppies are getting a little antsy. You know they were supposed to go to their new homes in four weeks, just before Christmas, and we've got Thanksgiving in a couple days…" I rattle on.

"Wow, always so much happening, isn't there?" Lynn asks, her sweet Canadian accent coming in strong.

"Isn't that the truth. Well, I am pulling up my Facebook and my emails to see if there is any response on my posting about the puppies. Oh, hold on…looks like there might be something." I click on an email with the subject "Missing puppies."

Hi Kate,

I saw your post about the missing puppies, and I wanted to let you know I saw a person fitting your description carrying a cardboard box into an apartment. Here is the address…

"Lynn!" I say. "I've got to go. I think we found the pups!"

"Okay, I'll await your update," Lynn says. "Praying for good news!"

I hang up and call Officer Sherman. "Officer! I got an email. I'm forwarding it to you as we speak!"

"All right, ma'am, my partner and I will check this out and keep you updated. Stay near a phone," the officer instructed.

"Will do. Thank you!"

I hang up the phone and call Alan. "Babe! I got an email lead and called Officer Sherman. He is headed over to the address right now to check it out. Is Jessica there with you?"

"No, I'm at my office downtown. That *is* great news! Want me to call her?" Alan asks.

"No, that's okay. I think I'm going to run home and stay with her until we get the call," I answer.

"Okay, sounds good. See, babe. I knew everything would work out."

*****

I pull into the driveway and run up the steps. I left Molly home with Jessica and Sapphire because she is an excellent emotional support dog, always has been.

"Jessica!" I call out. "We got a lead. The officer is checking it out as we speak and should call soon with an update."

"That's such a relief, Mom," Jessica says. "I can't believe someone responded so fast!"

"Well, sweetie, do you remember when you were little and the tattoo shop near my coffee shop got broken into? The owner had the thief on camera and posted it online and asked people to help keep an eye out. Your dad saw the post and spotted the guy wearing the tattoo shop's sweatshirt at the gas station and called it in. This is the beauty of social media: everything happens so much quicker because you have more eyes out there."

"Yeah, I sort of remember. That's how you got your first tattoo, right?" Jessica asks.

"Yep! That's how it happened. Why don't we bake some cookies while we wait for the phone call?" I suggest.

"Sounds good, Mom. Can we make some dog treats too? I want to have something for Sapphire and the pups when they are reunited."

"Of course! How about peanut butter bacon?" I ask.

"Sounds perfect! Thanks, Mom."

"No problem, sweetie."

I pull her close. It never stops shocking me when I hug my taller-than-me daughter.

After dinner, my phone finally rang. I looked at the caller ID, and it was Officer Sherman.

"Hello?" I answer timidly.

"Kate, I have good news! Your informant was right on. We found the perp and the pups. We are bringing the pups over in a few. We'll see you soon," says Officer Sherman.

"Yay! They found the pups! They are coming home!" I share with Alan and Jessica. "I better update on social media really quick while we wait for the officer."

"Good call, Mom," says Jessica. "I'm going to go get the treats we made them earlier."

4

As a rule, I generally take good care of myself. I consider myself healthy. I work out, I eat healthy and nutritious foods (without sacrificing the "yum factor"), I take time to rest when I need it, and I do things that feed my soul. I am a generally happy person with an optimistic outlook on life with the gift of encouragement.

Yet I find myself every so often needing to completely let loose, sleep in, have pizza *and* a bag of chips, stay in my pajamas, and shut out the world. Grief. Depression. Anxiety. Whatever you want to call it. It has no schedule. It is not a respecter of persons. It does not check with your personal assistant to see if you can fit it in to your day, week, or month.

Thankfully, I have a planned day off today. I can rest and have a reset while I allow my emotions to sift through the craziness of the last few months. Thanksgiving was great. We were all extra thankful for the miracle of the found pups. We snuck each of them a bit of turkey, and they were delighted.

As much as I love running the inn, I sometimes prefer hosting gatherings in my home, around my large farmhouse table. Feeling the love, familiarity, and comfort of the faces gathered around me. My table was beautiful; not to boast, but one of my specialties is a well-set tablescape. The rich wood from a local fir tree, topped with an earthy linen table runner and lined with eucalyptus leaves, mini pumpkins, and ivory tapers in gold candleholders. Each setting had a gold charger, a carefully placed blue ceramic plate, a wineglass, and my good Kate Spade utensils—the ones that come out only for special occasions.

The food was good, the company was good, and the general attitude was, well, thankful. I found it hard to get back into the swing of things after that; thus, here I am today in one of my "off" days. Let's just turn on Netflix and call it a self-care day. Sounds like more of a socially acceptable term in this day and age.

I have got a freshly brewed cup of coffee in my favorite teal mug, and I'm wearing my soft shapeless gray pajamas and a pair of fuzzy socks. Alan is working in the city today, and Jessica is at school. I've got plenty of snacks in the pantry and am already thinking about what I want to have delivered for lunch—pizza or sushi? Thank God for online ordering! I am all set up to spend the rest of this day not having to see or talk to another human.

I used to feel guilty about taking a self-care day, but then I read something really inspiring: "Self-care is giving the world the best of you instead of giving them the rest of you." Since I strive for excellence, this stuck with me. How can I serve my customers, my clients, my friends, my family with excellence if I am not 100 percent? I mean, we get regular oil changes to maintain our vehicles, we charge our electronics when they are low, so why not ourselves?

Long story short, I no longer feel guilty and am incredibly grateful for the opportunity to take a recharge day. I think more people should try it; if not a day, try ten minutes every day. Turn off your phone and go outside, take a bubble bath, or grab yourself your favorite coffee and enjoy it somewhere that brings you peace.

Okay, I'll stop coaching you now. You can read on.

*****

Part of my self-care last night was making muffins for the inn's guests this morning. I absolutely love watching them enjoy my fresh-baked goods.

"More coffee, Mr. Reynolds?" I ask, as I flitter about the dining room refilling coffee cups.

"Yes, please, Kathy," Mr. Reynolds responds. "I'm also going to need you to stop making some delectable pastries for us. The airline is going to make me buy an extra ticket if I eat too many more!"

"Sorry, Mr. Reynolds, we must serve tasty treats here at Still Waters. It's one of our specialties." I laugh.

Mr. and Mrs. Reynolds are one of our favorite regulars at Still Waters Inn. They are originally from England, but their son, Benji, goes to college up here on the coast, so they like to stay here whenever they come to visit him.

"How's Ben doing at school?" I inquire.

"He is doing so well academically, but we do worry about him. I guess at some point you have to cut the apron strings and let go." Mrs. Reynolds sighed.

"Nothing harder than being a parent, is there, Mrs. Reynolds?" I ask.

Mrs. Reynolds shakes her head, and Mr. Reynolds squeezes her hand.

"I'm sure he is going to do great things," I assure them. "You both are wonderful parents, and he has a good head on his shoulders."

"Thank you, Kathy. You always know what to say to comfort us. One of the reasons we love staying here so much. We are just drawn to the peace in this place. It's like vacationing in a warm hug," Mrs. Reynolds says.

"That is so kind of you to say. Let me know if I can do anything else for you two," I choke out, attempting not to cry.

I feel so strongly about creating a peaceful and comforting atmosphere in this inn. To know that is what people are experiencing when they choose to stay here makes my spirit burst.

*****

Today, Alan and I have a lunch date to start planning the Marriage Weekend we are hosting at the inn. We got really lucky in our marriage. Together, we constantly pursued tools to help us when we didn't know what a healthy marriage really looked like and through that found ourselves helping other couples, both pre-married (as we like to call them) and married. Evolving from that, here we find ourselves innkeepers who loved to pour into other relationships; that is what birthed our Marriage Weekends here at the inn.

As I park outside of our favorite little Thai spot, I scope him out already at a table inside. I wave as I enter the door and come to a halt at our table, shoving off my layers.

"Brrr! Why is winter so cold again?" I ask jokingly.

"Right? Just be thankful we don't live somewhere truly cold, like Alaska. If we think it's cold in Northern California, we definitely couldn't handle it there," Alan teases.

I make a face and stick out my tongue. We live for humor and a little bantering in our marriage. Laughter is good for you—cleans out the pipes, or something like that.

After we order—chicken pad Thai for both, of course!—we dive right into planning.

"What do you have so far, babe?" I ask.

"February 14."

"February 14? February 14 what? Like for the date?" I ask.

"Yep!" Alan replies. "It's perfect. It's already the love day, *and* it falls on a weekend. Boom!"

"It's a little cheesy and cliché, don't you think?" I ask.

"That's the point. What better time to pour into your life than on national love day?" Alan says jokingly.

"Well, let's come back to the date. How about the other details. Are we going to do a teaching? If so, what topic? Are we going to have a guided activity?"

"Yes and yes. How about your favorite topic? Communication."

"I love communication. It's literally the most important tool in any relationship. You will have to pull me down off my soapbox if we teach on this topic!" I say, exaggerating.

"Good," Alan says. "I like seeing you all fiery and passionate about things. It's cute."

"Let's keep brainstorming about an activity and a date."

"I still say Valentine's weekend." Alan crosses his arms stubbornly.

"I'll think about it. It's also so soon. It doesn't give us a ton of time to plan and get the word out. It's Christmas. Valentine's Day is literally right around the corner. But I am starting to get a lot of ideas with centering it around that holiday. Okay! Let's come back to the date. How's your lunch?"

I quickly change the subject to give my brain a break.

*****

Lunch with Alan was so productive, and as hesitant as I am for doing a Valentines-themed Marriage Weekend, the ideas are starting to flood my brain, so I have been holed up in my office all afternoon getting it all out on paper. And I still need to finish my Christmas shopping tonight; Christmas is next week!

I stick my notebook and pen back in my desk drawer for the day and slip my coat back on, not quite ready to brave the holiday crowds at the mall. Nevertheless, "brave men did not kill dragons; brave men rode them." I don't actually know that this applies here, but I like to find poetry or good quotes to psyche myself up. Let's go!

The mall is exactly as I expected; maybe I would prefer riding a dragon over fighting through the crowds of people trying to find just the perfect gift. I think the food court is my first stop; who can shop without a boba tea and a corn dog first? Definitely not me, and definitely not tonight.

In case you haven't already deduced this for yourself, my brain is always in planning mode, so it shouldn't come as a surprise that while I'm Christmas shopping for the fam, I'm also thinking about the last-minute details for the inn. Decorating for Christmas (mostly all finished), making people feel special, and planning the tiny details are some of my favorite things. The joy of being able to do these things almost trumps the accompanied stress of the holidays in general—almost.

Now let's see. I've got baked goods and the hot cocoa bar covered, thanks to my talented teen. Finish putting together the Christmas stockings for our guests. Any guest who stays with us during the holidays gets extra treats during their stay; that is just a given. In each stocking, of course, will be a candy cane or two, a box of Band-Aids (practical), cozy and festive socks, and some other goodies I've collected from local vendors.

We have a tree by the front desk with RAK tags on them; each tag has an idea for a RAK—random act of kindness. We encourage each guest to grab and perform the RAK on their tag. Finally, the Sunday evening before Christmas, we gather around the piano and sing Christmas carols, and not only do we invite the guests but also open it up to the town.

5

Wild hogs.

Sometimes my life feels like a cartoon. Turkeys, racoons, squirrels, and even deer I've seen wandering around our town and property, but never have I ever thought I'd see this day.

Sometimes I'm surprised that I still get surprised by these things, but here they were, eighteen of those ugly things standing in the backyard! Most were young ones, but the real danger lies in the mama protecting her babies. You definitely don't want to get in her way; the term *Momma Bear* comes to mind. But even the babies have razor-sharp teeth!

Okay, this is starting to sound like a horror story, I agree. But I can assure you it is not; you will sleep soundly tonight. Well, I can't guarantee you won't dream of wild hogs. Lord knows I do from time to time, but I digress.

Luckily, after the holidays, it's a bit slow around the inn, so we didn't have many guests. I made sure to explain to the guest the predicament and request that no one try to be a hero; the last thing I needed was for a guest at my inn to have an injury because they were trying to wrangle a dozen wild hogs during their relaxing stay at Still Waters Inn. I also gave them a bit of a discount because when those hogs were around, it was anything but restful.

After dealing with some destruction of a few flower beds, I was able to find who to call to round these porkers up and get them off my property. A few helpful farmers came out and set up baited traps. These hogs were smart, though. We never knew when and where they were going to show up. I sent up a prayer of gratitude that there were no events booked for this week. Could you imagine if there had been a wedding? "I now pronounce you man and *oink*!" Not good.

One night, we were awakened at 3:00 a.m. by the sound of squealing pigs. I had been sleeping in one of the vacant rooms just in case we caught them in the middle of night. Sure enough, we did. The 250-pound momma and one of her young had been caught in the trap. Momma and baby squealed for freedom the rest of the morning.

The farmers came at daylight and removed them, and they received a new home—away from my inn. The following night, the rest came back, and the traps worked.

One of our guests jokingly declared, "Hogs gone wild!"

I was only slightly amused but grateful to be rid of the wild hogs.

*****

"Hi, Doug!" I say. "Beautiful morning, isn't it?"

Doug is our groundskeeper/gardener. He's a perfectionist and likes things to be just so. I always find him out in the yard fixing, planting, watering, uprooting something. He keeps the outside as beautiful if not more so than the inside.

"It's a great morning to be replanting these tulips that got trampled by those crazy hogs," he replied. "I'm just glad there wasn't more damage to my perfect yard."

"You are a godsend for fixing those flowers up so quickly. With Alan's surprise birthday barbecue coming up in a couple of weeks, I'm glad to be rid of those hogs and have a beautiful outdoor space again."

"You should have kept one of those hogs," Doug suggested. "Not in my flower beds, of course, but I'm sure it would have been really yummy on a spit at the barbecue."

"Gross," I replied. "No, thank you. You just leave the food to Nikki and me, and we'll leave the plants to you."

"Sounds good." He laughed. "But just think about how much it would have saved you on meat!"

Doug chuckled to himself as he worked on the flowers. I walked away totally disgusted. I love bacon as much as the next person, but I'm more of a gatherer than a hunter. If we were left to our own devices to come up with food, I'd be a forced vegetarian. Most likely due to the fact that I would name whatever animal I caught and then would be unable to do the killing needed for the eating. Probably make them a cute little sweater. Possibly a matching hat...

*****

"Hey, Nikki, did we need to finalize any of the menu for Alan's birthday barbecue?" I ask, as I walk straight to the coffeepot.

"Hi, Kate, how are you today?" Nikki asks. "Would you like a cup of coffee? Or maybe I could just grab a funnel and pour it down your throat." A gigantic grin spreads across her freckled face.

"Ha ha, you're so funny." I roll my eyes "I do apologize for my zombielike need for coffee that forces me to abandon all polite niceties. Please, Nikki, tell me. How are you today?" I say playfully as I sip my coffee.

"Anyway, to answer your earlier question, check this out!" Nikki throws back a tablecloth that was covering her normally clear workstation to reveal all of Alan's favorites and everything you could want for a barbecue.

There were barbecue ribs (his all-time fave), baked beans, corn on the cob, potato salad, among a few other tasty-looking dishes.

"I wanted to do a test run to make sure everything came out good," Nikki says.

"It looks and smells like heaven, but what are you going to do with all this food?" I ask.

"I already called the homeless shelter, and I'm going to wrap it up and take it over when I'm done serving breakfast," replies Nikki.

I threw my arms around Nikki. "You are both hilarious and extremely generous—two of my favorite qualities in a friend."

It looks like Alan's birthday barbecue is all set for next weekend. Hopefully, it will make up for last year's birthday fail. I got him a paint kit. You'd think I'd know a man better than that after being married for almost twenty years! But no, I had to get him the most un-*Alan*-like gift there ever was.

I'm usually pretty spot-on at gifts, but I guess we all make mistakes at one time or another. He laughed about it but has not let me live it down all year. Even at Christmas, where I totally won the gift game, he still brought up the birthday fail. Isn't it great that I surround myself with sarcastically funny people everywhere I go?

The law of attraction: like attracts like. Be a loving person, and the universe will send you more people, things, and experiences to love. Be a hateful person, and you know what's going to happen!

*****

January 27. It's here. Today is the day—the day to redeem myself to my husband as the ultimate gift giver! I grab my royal blue sweater because it's still chilly outside, and it's his favorite color.

Look at that, I'm already winning! I say to myself.

I chuckle as I put on some makeup and do my hair.

I head to the kitchen to make Alan a birthday breakfast complete with French toast (with loads of powdered sugar), bacon, and fresh fruit. After a quick yet enjoyable breakfast with the family, I run over to the inn to do some quick work before the big barbecue starts.

As I pull up to the inn, I can see everyone already hard at work: Doug perfecting our already perfect lawn, Mitchell—my front desk / assistant manager—arranging the lawn furniture, and Nikki's kitchen staff setting up the grill and outdoor kitchen.

I walk into the kitchen as Nikki is finishing up breakfast for the guests.

"Good morning, Kate," Nikki greets me. "Are you hungry? We have extra this morning."

"I'm good, thanks. Just finished birthday breakfast with the fam. Just came in to check on the krackle I made last night for Alan."

"Oh, that's right," Nikki responds. "All right, I'll leave you to it. There is fresh coffee in the pot."

"You are a saint."

Krackle is a tradition; it's also Alex's favorite dessert. It consists of saltine crackers topped with homemade caramel and melted chocolate chips. He loves it, so do most people. I've heard many a people refer to it as actual crack. But it's not my cup of tea. A little too sweet and rich for me. I'm more of a savory gal myself.

*****

"You guys, this is amazing!" Alan exclaims. "All my favorite people and my favorite foods combined in one place for me. This is crazy! Thank you to everyone who made this happen, and thank you to my beautiful wife who was behind all of it. I can't wait for my other birthday present when we get home."

He winks my way, and the crowd sends out a chorus of catcalls.

Leave it to my sweet husband to make things slightly inappropriate.

As I bask in my victory of ultimate gift giver, queen birthday celebrator (pardon me as I get carried away in my humility), and party hostess with the mostest, I'm approached by someone I've never seen before. He is carrying a plate but wearing a very snazzy suit. Must be a business contact of Alex's. But I thought I knew everyone on the guest list.

"Kate? I'm Donald Brooks, friend of your husband's," he introduced himself. "We are in the same investors mastermind group."

"Nice to meet you, Donald. I hope you're enjoying the party. Do you need any refreshments?" I ask, ever the hostess.

"Oh, I am just fine, thank you. I wanted to speak with you about your inn. You have such a charming little place here. Alan told me it's 80 percent booked most of the year. That's incredible!"

"Thank you. This is a dream come true for me. I've always wanted to own and operate my own inn. How about you? What do you do, Donald? What kind of investments?" I ask to make polite conversation.

"Well, Kate, that's what I wanted to talk to you about. How would you feel about owning and operating multiple inns, just like the one you have here, Still Waters?" Donald asked.

I smile to myself and think about a quote from one of my favorite books: "If it matters to you, it matters to Him." It reminds me of God's goodness. I mean, really, how could I forget?

"The Lord is my rock, my fortress and deliver; my God is my rock, in whom I take refuge, my shield and the horn of my salvation, my stronghold" (Psalm 18:2).

The End

To find out what happens next, follow author Kathy Branning for her next book in the series.

Recipe for krackle on next page.

RECIPE FOR KRACKLE

- 1 1/2 sleeve saltine crackers
- 1 1/4 cups butter
- 1 1/4 cups brown sugar
- 1 1/2 cups chocolate chips (I prefer dark chocolate)

Instructions:

1. Preheat oven to 325°F. Line a rimmed baking sheet with foil; spray with cooking spray (trust me on this). Line with saltine crackers, placing them real close. I wind up with six rows of eight crackers.
2. In a medium saucepan, bring butter and brown sugar to a boil over medium-high heat. Let it bubble for 3 minutes, then remove from the heat and pour evenly over the crackers. Spread with back of spoon to fill any gaps.
3. Place in oven, and bake for 10 minutes until golden.
4. Remove from the oven. Scatter chocolate chips on top while the caramel is still warm. Tent the chocolate with aluminum foil to trap the heat and ensure even melting. Let sit for 10 minutes, then spread chocolate chips with back of metal spoon. (Optional: I like to use festive sprinkles of whatever holiday I'm making them for and sprinkle on top of melted chocolate before freezing.)
5. Let cool completely on countertop, then stick in freezer for 2–3 hours until solid. Break into pieces, and store in fridge or freezer.

ABOUT THE AUTHOR

Kathy Branning was born and raised in Southern California. Kathy and her family have adopted a small town in beautiful Northern California as their new home—near lakes, waterfalls, and lots of glorious trees!

Kathy uses her writing to process grief, experience and to share healing with her readers. She hopes you are inspired and uplifted as you follow her characters on their journey through family reconciliation, grief, self-exploration, friendship, faith, hope, and love.

Kathy considers her faith and family to be most important to her. If she isn't spending time with her friends and family, you can almost always find her around her sweet bichon-Maltese mix, Snow.

'Tis So Suite: Tales of an Innkeeper is Kathy's first published book.

CPSIA information can be obtained
at www.ICGtesting.com
Printed in the USA
BVHW040651290522
638400BV00019B/159

9 781685 700966